Transmission Loss

To John, with gratitude for your warm and
wise presence around the Parkhurst. I hope
you find something here that speaks to you!

Chelsea

Transmission Loss

Chelsea Jennings

University of Massachusetts Press
Amherst and Boston

Copyright © 2018 by Chelsea Jennings
All rights reserved
Printed in the United States of America

ISBN 978-1-62534-339-0 (paper)

Designed by Sally Nichols
Set in Alexina
Printed and bound by Maple Press Inc.

Cover design by CPorter Designs, llc
Cover art: William Henry Fox Talbot, *Photomicrograph of moth wings*, c. 1840

Library of Congress Cataloging-in-Publication Data
A catalog record for this book is available from the Library of Congress.

British Library Cataloguing-in-Publication Data
A catalog record for this book is available from the British Library.

Contents

Transmission Loss

I

TONIGHT THE TREES

are braiding each other's branches. *Sister, sister.*
I sit at the sewing table, working
the treadle of a dead machine. What about

the cold suggests an absence, distance? In winter
the bedroom's too big, the heart's a root,
a beet, earth-in-the-earth. Outside the window,

apples fall hard and startle the lavender.
Under a finger—*phosphorous, lucifer, fire-inch-stick*—
summer's as small as the head of a match.

HEIRLOOM

As close to the past as maps can get to rivers
A boat full of stones   A handful of water

*

This is the dressmaker's frame
where we hang our fear of the dark

Again and again we thread it
though the eye of sleep is small

*

It could have been a locket with a lock of hair inside
It could have been a mirror   A set of silver   A coin

*

There was a pewter cup and a patron saint
for each of the children who lived

They kept their records in the Bible
They shared a single bridal dress

*

This is the watchmaker's shop
where the balance wheel can be fixed

*

We wear their scrimshaw earrings
and are called by their given names

We dream that we're drowning   We dream that
we wake   And we eat our meals from their plates

LANDSCAPE WITHOUT THE FALL OF ICARUS

Skeins of smoke in the sky
The cornfields suffer snow

Moon, barn, bird, as in
a photogram: objects

exposed as layered light
Love as a joint into which

a little blood has leaked
(scissors, a straight pin

a pair of hands) And why
not cry in the root cellar?

Loose ice in the wind, grief
freezes and falls through the air

HISTORY OF PHOTOGRAPHY

If the subject of every photograph is time

The light changes on the Boulevard
du Temple

The denizens of Paris walk freely through
history's frame

*

You have a famous memory O friend
O photographer

You have a knack for shadows

Your buildings look like nudes

*

Of early pictures: *very perfect*
but extremely small

A latticed window in which is visible
each diamond of glass

If the frame is the subject of photography

*

The streets of time are empty

You stand as still as a photograph

The window opens on nostalgia and the light
keeps moving past

THE STATIONS OF THE CROSS: LEMA SABACHTHANI

Barnett Newman
Magna, oil, acrylic, and Duco on canvas
1958–1966

1

Wind freezes in the grass.
Even the sun turns white.

The austere, the interior
season, the year a reliquary

holding that pebble of bone.

2

Threadbare clouds, colorless sky—
A cold so narrow only the heart can move—

3

This is not a window that
looks out onto the visible silence

of a field where the hay
has been cut and cleared.

4

Not the door through which
one could enter the flat, lambent,

medieval scene of crucifixion

with its cracked brushwork
and the reassurance of angels.

5

A procession of days without weather.

Branches drifting through sky,
time, dragging an empty net.

6

What little happens suffices.
The cord of water poured

from the kettle, the seam
of light that surrounds the door.

7

Each hour can hold
so much snow. Morning lasts

all morning, the trees stand
motionless in stone gowns.

8

Here is tragedy threshed from
chronology. The quality of a story.

9

In brightness with no vanishing point

who can say whether sorrow
is the greater or the lesser white.

10

On the pilgrimage from one end
of winter to the other

unseen deer drop antlers
into the snow.

11

The landscape on a human scale,
but empty. Ice grips the ground,

brush huddles at the edge
of perspective.

12

Evening brims its banks,
closes one distance to open another.

13

This is not a mirror covered
with cloth, a surface

in which darkness changes direction.

14

When the stars behind the stars
come out, they perforate the sky

until there's nothing left
but a field of light.

INSOMNIA: OSSUARY

Sheared from the soul
>> at last the skull

can be polished and sorted
>> the long bones laid

in rows (repetition is
>> beauty's terrain)

With one hand locked
>> in the other

I stack my knees
>> I count the bones in my feet

HAPTICS

Statue of Eirene
Roman copy of Greek original by Kephisodotos
Marble
c. 14–68
Metropolitan Museum of Art

Pillar of cloth as tall as a woman
with the perfect polished foot, breast

that survives the head, pure core,
the archetypal fragment. To know

one's own position in space, to move
in the direction of meaning, the idea of

an arm extended from the shoulder's
broken socket. As if what the hand knows

could be held in the hand. That the marble
flutes of fabric are what the figure is.

HOAR FROST

Sun filters through the frozen air.
A pair of horses stands in a field

of mist suspended as if their breath.
A higher order of silence, a way white

overthrows the world. Each birch
relieved of singularity, each beam

of the fence. A landscape already
in memory's language:

numberless branches, unbroken snow,
the perfect composure of the horses.

TRUE BLACK

Untitled works
Lee Bontecou
Welded steel, canvas, fabric, wire
1959–1962

Into the anthracite
the bone-char dark

Into the lustrous
birdless inner night

*

Warm or cool
Empty or overfull

All black is a theory of black

*

What do we see when we think
we see absence

For there is the question of brilliance

Whether matte or shiny
polished or rough

*

The harder we look the more
black absorbs us

The canvas approaches
with its own pupil wide

*

The harder we look the more
darkness dilates

A sky widespread in each aperture

*

When the armature of art contains
a burnt-out endlessness

How turn toward it
How turn away

BABYLONIAN MAP OF THE WORLD

enough abstraction and the world will fit
in one hand : not navigable but small enough

to encompass : a landmass ringed by a river
of bitter water : an ocean that reaches an ocean

of sky : a place inhabited by language : names
of impossible beasts : ruined cities : ruined gods

inside the sea : every map ends somewhere :
the past is a country beyond the reach of birds

II

PRISM: INVOCATION

Here in the darkened chamber
the polished surface of the sun
splits into syntax / *Scattered*
and gathered / *Seven names*
for the same light / Here
white's thread is never lost /
Here the concept or logic of
white stands in the middle of
the   visible   world

THE INVENTION OF BLUE

Before blue blindness
fell at dusk

Clouds composed the sky

Before blue sun never
entered water

Distance fit into a window

*

Blue came last as it was
                    an ending

A pose night took until
                    the gold was gone

*

Then on the ocean's grey waves
came ultramarine

Blue had been a species of darkness

Now applied as pure pigment
it tore a hole in the world

*

Blue had existed in dreams of course

This color beside which life
appears ashen

*

Blue that shines in the shadows

Brightens the milk

Makes room
for the lead-white daylight to fill

ALPINE LAKE

A cold that rings the bone
Presses the heat to the heart

A body   we say   of water

Sun insists on the lake
The shadows still gather snow

Stillness a substance of such magnitude

we step out into   The mind
contracts to its branch of nerves

As bare sky spreads across the water

SAINT FRANCIS PREACHES TO THE BIRDS

Attributed to Giotto
Fresco
c. 1296–1304
Basilica Papale di San Francesco

More than anything: his hands.
The air around them stays blue
so they move in their own

atmosphere. The birds let in light
but his hands are real wings.
The birds leave their tree and his hands

are loosed to regard the world
in their way. His voice a gold disc,
a halo of sound. The birds listen

and nearly disappear. Heaven is there
in the measure of his hands,
opening and shutting like a bird.

ON THE STEPS OF THE SEATTLE ASIAN ART MUSEUM

The eye's octave of color must widen
from pitch-grey to indigo-jet.
How else to account for the crow?

*

Beak black as a ritual dagger,
wings black as the bones of a fan.

*

They settle on Noguchi's *Black Sun,*
reduce it to a hoop of gunmetal,
to the dim ring of granite that it is.

*

The sun overhead is a color wheel,
giving such saturation to the crow.

*

How easily the light flew through
the wires of that nineteenth-century
ornamental birdcage.

VIRIDIAN

Mont Sainte-Victoire
Paul Cézanne
Oil on canvas
1902–1904

The wildness of all the earth
organized by green, a grammar

of color. The landscape beneath
the landscape is geometry: the eyes

touch everything twice. In what
we call *the field of vision* every line

is a horizon, the grass a pigment
that brightens as we grind it.

CLEAR GLASS

1

Transparent but watery
as looking into or out of a dream

the window demands certain purities
of matter

Centuries spent clarifying sand
into absence

2

Clear glass frames the wind
working its way through a tree

On this substance the sun shows
none of its usual restraint

3

Flawless and solid as lacquered rain
the pane is set apart from history

It takes a certain thickness of glass
to put the moment plainly

4

The window is an opening to admit weather

wind-aperture   wind-eye

and glass merely a way of glazing the view

The viridescent day presses against it
feeling around for a way through

WAVE / PARTICLE

This world / being both / is not our world

A realm where matter moves otherwise
Everything behaves like light —

From time to time it feels like this: that

the self is a conjecture beyond which
there is nothing / else

The ghost of a face on a clear surface:
a language we all speak: attenuation

This world / being both / cannot be believed

Though dust in the air makes light appear
as it is // particulate

The window divides the sun and the odds
are perfect every time

Light strikes glass / some of it scatters

We know how it ends once it's over

INSOMNIA: PULSE

I lie on the heart's side
    Sounding out the night

The ring of a shovel on rock
    Digging a garden
    Digging a grave

If I sleep I will dream
    My heart has flown from me

Through a window
    As dark as a wall

WAKING BEFORE DAWN IN A SMALL HOUSE NOT OUR OWN

on whose steep roof rain has written in italics
until our dreams are made of water

night and rain the same soft cloth
even the field tucked in at the corners

no other sound in the drowned grass
into the seedpod the self each creature gathers

stranded half-sleeping in time's pocket
waiting for daylight to wave its blue banner

NORTHBOUND TRAIN

Seattle–Vancouver

River of wind through trees

The sea and the sky trade
greys

This place a verge

*

Rain collecting on a pane of glass

To have spent the winter
on the inside of a cloud —

*

At last   At least

The weight of your hand
on my heart

Slow sway as the train
picks up speed

*

Northward into negative space

Point of the needle
Arrow of geese

*

On a coastline that only exists
at this hour

Nothing at the periphery

but the ocean's salt-light

*

A distant ship's whistle—
Pillars of vanished piers—

      In memory of

*

The heartwood is the hardest timber

A ring for every year

*

Your breath against the window
disappears and disappears

The clouds drift elsewhere

The trees keep raining

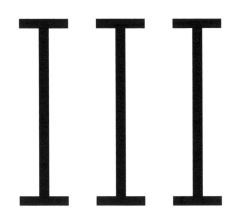

BEFORE THE INVENTION OF PERSPECTIVE IN PAINTING

The sword and the sky are contiguous,
the halo of one saint the face of another.

Every leaf on the tree turns to be seen.
Angels never fall through the uneven

azurite, the hand stays grafted to the heart.
Devotion is possible. No thing behind

the color of a rock. Gold stops at the garment,
touches it, touches what skin is exposed.

Now mother and child need only one body.
The impossible bowl of wine will not spill.

TRANSMISSION LOSS

The dead speak to us on the radio
in their native voices   Lower

and lower the frequency
The signal thin with static

*

The postcard is not the ocean
The note on the verso is not

the beloved   Deep in a suitcase
two teacups are crushed

*

The lens can focus from infinity
to a meter   The camera contains

one woman   Her face overwritten
with her own skittish hair

ETYMOLOGY OF YELLOW

Where the roads run straight and long
and the orderly fields show the shape
of the land, wind moves in from the distant
present, the acres of canola shudder
like sunlight, it hurts to regard so much
of a single color (the mind itself in flower),
this, the only yellow on earth
                —*bright and shining, crying out*

BLACK AND WHITE PHOTOGRAPHY

Lella, Bretagne, 1947
Edouard Boubat
Silver gelatin print

Light takes up all the space

The sky striations   imperfections
in the sun   The ocean overbright

*

So all that's here belongs to the past

The first principle of light
That it arrives a little too late

*

Color had been an afterthought
anyway   White sleeves

Her unbleached dress catching wind

*

Blinded by her blown hair

Her absolute shadow behind her
in the sand

*

The rest of the darkness kept
underfoot   So all that's here is

each texture radiance takes

*

Brightness that gives the air
a kind of grain   Nearly

erases the row of broken waves

*

On the strand between afterwards
and emptiness

How unlike light light is

SHADES OF ORANGE

Adriatic
Helen Frankenthaler
Acrylic on canvas
1968

The sun sets all at once. The world
goes orange and stays that way.
Orange soaks, spills over, *burnt, persimmon,*
still we have no name for the sun
that stains the dusk-violet strip of sea.

*

Anything large will immerse you or serve
as scenery. *So what do you do with the corners
of pictures?* There is nowhere else
to go. Orange, an empire of sorrow.
The closer you stand the greater the scale.

COSMOLOGY: EXPANSION

Even in summer the stars shiver / silver our hair

Bounded by a silence that increases with time
We spread a blanket beneath them

> As every star drifts farther apart
> We are left with the moon / whose weight we drag

But tonight the universe is not inscrutable
Nothing rushes away from its center / for now

Our backs are pressed against the ground

SELF-PORTRAIT AS JACOB WRESTLING
THE ANGEL

Because it came in the guise
of a moth   a white moth

ticking at the ceiling   flying
to and from the lamp

in what appeared to be a language
and later   to be panic

I could not tell what it wanted
and waited a long time to open

the curtain   to let it leave
a hole in the wool of the evening

RAIN

erases the rain that came before,
forcing us inward, into the thought
of the storm, into the rooms

whose windows stream with seamless
water, where our sorrows, our errors,
seek shelter. An ordinary day contains us,

raises a wall of rain around the hours.
Branches scrape at the attic,
the shattered plums lie where they fall.

INSOMNIA: LABYRINTH

Under a corridor of stars
    Everywhere is familiar

        The moon moves closer
    The color of broken stone

What part of the dream
    Is only a dream

        (No great beast within)
    (No spool of thread)

Dragging one hand along the wall
    Turning the same direction

        Again and again

SWIMMING IN THE DARK

Night ripens in the bramble.
A true wheel turns the constellations.

Effortlessly we possess these bodies,
each in her windchamber. The sky

deepens in all directions, a darkness
embroidered by branches. Black

fabric, black thread. Black a season
unto itself, with room enough

for all our losses. Migratory shadows
in a downpour of stars.

.

IV

SHIFT

Everywhere we see ourselves : the clothesline's
cotton nightgown : a change of position
or wind : nervy sleeves that cast their shadows
on our sleep : At times the ghost is just
a shift : an empty thing pinned between trees :
but always arriving : always breathless

FALL

Deciduous mood. Winter descends on the threads
of a screw. The wind is full of undifferentiated feeling,
the day's heat on its way out of the house.

Some spiritual presence, or some disturbance
of the ocular nerve, throws knives of light into one
corner of the room. Sun streams through the cinch

in an hourglass. Sun like salt, like sand. In this weather,
laundry surrenders. A window swings on its singing hinge,
someone sweeps the walk with a hard-bristled broom.

SELF-PORTRAIT IN X RAYS

From the body's darkness, with beautiful distinctness,
the shoulder with its animal architecture intact.

Not even a minor fracture. And here is the habit
of standing, lift in the left wing of the pelvic bone,

the heavy skull held at a tilt. A slash, a shadow,
marks the heart. *Is the invisible visible? Not to the eye,*

but its results are: a compass needle seen through
the closed brass cover, coins through a calico pocket.

SLEEPING ALONE

Night arrives in large-format, a dark cloth
        to cover the shoulders and face. The square of a dream
            the only way to see out.

Your image on the ground glass: dim as if viewed
        through water or a thin sheet of smoke, the brightness
            falling off at the edges.

This long exposure to an inner landscape,
        this moment in the right light that lasts—
           hold still, hold still.

INSOMNIA: GABRIEL

Awakened by a voice as simple as birdsong

     I am here   *I am here*   *Here I am*

Left to listen to the blood in the head

(Longing to be lifted up
                  and set back down again)

ILLUMINATION

scribes with frozen hands
compose the past
               squinting
into days that never break

the hand is perfect but the eye
will lose its place
               words fall
forever through these openings

            [*lacuna: a puncture, a gap, a little lake, a hollow*]

still the scribes go on singing
and praying the hours
               smoothing
the parchment with a stone

over and over they shape
the same letters
               with everywhere
these flecks of hammered gold

VERMILION

A nothing-other-than, a red
that robs the world. A perfect
assurance that no part of love
is easy, not even the body is ours.

The garment overtakes us.
The heart is a handful of glass
for this flame. Observe how
the angels turn their faces away.

SELF-PORTRAIT AS A BIRD'S NEST

Summer's brocade falls and all that's left
is a small expression of effort

a coarse bowl built from the inside
when every bush seemed to sing

only woven twigs among twigs
a leaf-scarred structure of empty-

handedness that continues into autumn
chancing the elements

THE HUMAN FIGURE IN MOTION

Eadweard Muybridge
Collotypes
1872–1885

1
So much of life is spent with the weight
on the wrong foot. So much of love

is someone walking toward or away
at ordinary speed. A dress struggled into

or removed, water poured from one vessel
to another. Moment by moment

2
we survive our desire. A woman arches
into a scarf or pulls on a stocking, leans back

in a chair with a cigarette. Abandons herself
into we know not what, closing her eyes

on her thoughts. The smoke loosens,
the fabric blooms, time is divided

3
into increments we can manage. Time
is a grid, a square of squares. Day after day

we sweep the same floor, lift the same cup
to the lips. At night we lay ourselves down

on the usual side. Love as it ends breaks
our habits, there are small sudden changes

4
between frames: a shift in the hip, a variation
on the deep private expression of the face.

Memory runs in reverse, water returns
to the pitcher. The woman on the staircase

turns to face the camera, the human figure
coming in and out of focus.

PETRICHOR

Rain lays down the dust

Live water finding its way
back into the rock

A mineral quality to the air

as it travels from room to room
shutting doors

So this is grief then

Rain falls on the leafmeal
with a *hush*

Wind that enters the house

The smell of earth that rises
from the earth

ELEGY

bird in the shirtpocket   heart of my heart
bird on a wire no mortal can cross

bird in the thicket   thorn for a beak
bird shook loose from history's sleeve

bird that gives a dark shape to the dark
still as the stone of saint anthony's arm

nest in the attic   snow in the nest
a bird the only leaf on the branch

bird that flies from the past to the past
bird in the tree in the cage of the breast

Notes

"History of Photography"

"I had very small boxes made, in which I fixed lenses of shorter focus, and with these I obtained very perfect but extremely small pictures." —William Henry Fox Talbot, "Some Account of the Art of Photogenic Drawing"

"True Black"

"Black is an abstraction; there is no black, only black things. . . . But they are black in different ways, for there is the question of brilliance, whether they are matte or shiny, polished, rough, fine, and so forth." —Jean DuBuffet, "The Common Man at Work"

"Babylonian Map of the World"

"the rui[ned] cities"; "the ruined gods which he [settled] inside the Sea"; "A winged [bi]rd cannot safely compl[ete its journey]." —translation of writing on the Babylonian map of the world, from Wayne Horowitz, "The Babylonian Map of the World"

"'river' of 'bitter' water." —translation of writing on the Babylonian map of the world, from Michael Kerrigan, *The Ancients in Their Own Words*

"Prism"

"What is the impression of white, what is the meaning of this expression, what is the logic of this concept 'white'?"; "Would it be correct to say our concepts reflect our life? They stand in the middle of it." —Ludwig Wittgenstein, *Remarks on Colour*

"Shades of Orange"

"What do you do with corners of pictures." —Helen Frankenthaler, oral history interview, Archives of American Art, Smithsonian Institution

"Self-Portrait in X Rays"
"The bones of the fore legs show with beautiful distinctness."
—Cleveland Moffett, "The Röntgen Rays in America," *McClure's,* April 1896

"'Is the invisible visible?' 'Not to the eye; but its results are'"; "A photograph of a compass showed the needle and dial taken through the closed brass cover"; "Cork-screw, key, pencil with metallic protector, and piece of coin, as photographed while inside a calico pocket."
—H. J. W. Dam, "The New Marvel in Photography," *McClure's,* April 1896

"History of Photography" owes a debt to Geoffrey Batchen's *Each Wild Idea: Writing, Photography, History.*

Several poems in this collection, particularly "The Invention of Blue," draw on Philip Ball's *Bright Earth: Art and the Invention of Color.*

Acknowledgments

My grateful acknowledgment to the editors of the publications in which these poems first appeared:

Boston Review: "Landscape without the Fall of Icarus,"
"Before the Invention of Perspective in Painting"
Cincinnati Review: "Elegy"
december: "Heirloom"
Madison Review: "Tonight the Trees"
Make It True: Poetry from Cascadia: "Fall," "Swimming in the Dark"
Mississippi Review: "On the Steps of the Seattle Asian Art Museum"
Sugar House Review: "Transmission Loss"

Warm thanks to James Haug and Dara Wier for believing in the manuscript and Mary Dougherty, Sally Nichols, Dawn Potter, and the University of Massachusetts Press for so gracefully transforming it into a book.

I thank my many teachers for their wisdom and kindness, especially Jody Bolz and David McAleavey, who urged me onward at a crucial time; Jessica Burstein, who sharpened my thinking about poetry and so much else; and Andrew Feld and Brian Reed, who pointed the way forward to these poems. Thanks also to my students, for keeping me connected to the inner workings of language.

I am profoundly grateful to my brothers, Brett and Chaz Jennings, for championing my writing (and me in general); and to my parents, Mo and Bob Jennings, for keeping faith in me, for encouraging me to run free in both my imagination and the woods behind our house and, in my father's case, for letting me gradually ransack his personal library.

Most of all, I am grateful to Heather Arvidson, my best editor and my companion in all things, for making a life that makes poetry possible.

JUNIPER
JUNIPER PRIZE FOR POETRY

This volume is the forty-third recipient of the
Juniper Prize for Poetry, established in 1975 by the
University of Massachusetts Press in collaboration with
the UMass Amherst MFA program for Poets and Writers.
The prize is named in honor of the poet Robert Francis
(1901–1987), who for many years lived in Fort Juniper,
a tiny home of his own construction, in Amherst.